Spacebaby

HENRIETTA BRANFORD
Illustrated by Ellis Nadler

Collins

An Imprint of HarperCollins*Publishers*

First published in Great Britain by Collins in 1996
First published in paperback by Collins in 1997
Collins is an imprint of HarperCollins *Publishers* Ltd
77-85 Fulham Palace Road, Hammersmith, London, W6 8JB

5 7 9 8 6

Text copyright © Henrietta Branford 1996
Illustrations copyright © Ellis Nadler 1996

ISBN 0 00 675175 X

The author and illustrator assert the moral right
to be identified as the author and illustrator of the work.

Printed and bound in Great Britain by
Caledonian International Book Manufacturing Ltd,
Glasgow G64

CONTENTS

For my daughter Rose Carter.
And for Ann-Janine Murtagh –
this book is all her fault.

1 Giant Frisbee

Tipperary was camping with Hector on Mount Wrath the night I arrived. They'd finished supper – fried egg sandwiches, Hector's favourite – and they were sitting by the fire.

Tipperary was working on some **BIPS** (Bus Improvement Plans) for her **SOFTIE** (Super-de luxe Family Travel Experience). Hector had finished licking the frying pan and was having a scratch.

Suddenly the wind got up and blew the clouds across the moon. The sky went black, the clouds unzipped and the rain came down in spouts. Tipperary saw a circle of light coming in over the mountains, spinning like a giant frisbee.

Hector shot down inside the sleeping bag and hid. He says he didn't but I bet he did. Tipperary stuck her head out of the tent. She stood up with the wind blowing her hair and the rain soaking her jacket and watched as the giant frisbee dropped down, lighting up the mountain.

It stopped just below the summit, humming and thrumming. The light intensified and the frisbee began to skim down the valley, turning the pine trees violet, indigo, azure, emerald, golden, orange and ruby red.

The noise dropped. The colours faded. The frisbee vanished. Tipperary stood outside the tent with water dripping off her hood and stared at nothing. She felt as though a lovely present had been pulled out of her hand.

Then she heard me. She says I sounded small and angry.

2 Hello, Treasure

I lay in the dark, feeling horrible. Every time I opened my mouth a noise like a siren came out of it. My nose blocked up, I couldn't breathe and my head wobbled.

Suddenly a whiskery cold-nose thing with an eye on each side pushed itself at me. A terrible wet smell blasted me. Something hot and slobbery shot out and wiped my face. I shut my eyes and cried as loudly as I could. It seemed to be the only thing that I was good at.

Two big boots crashed down, one on each side of me. Two strong hands took hold of me. One slid under my bum, the other curved behind my head.

"Hello, treasure," someone said. Those were the first words I heard on Earth. "Hello, treasure."

The hands picked me up, tucked me in somewhere warm and dark, and ran with me. Something soft was wrapped around me. I opened my eyes and saw Tipperary.

That was a shock – I didn't know what Earth mothers looked like till I saw Tipperary. She has nice orange hair, but only on her head. She has big round eyes – just two – and two pink ears with rings in. She has two arms and two legs, and some bits in between. She's all different colours and she's got a big wide smile.

When I saw Hector I couldn't believe my eyes. My private name for Earth beings is *twobies*, because I've noticed they have two of most things. Not Hector though. I'd never seen anything like Hector. He has short hair all over *including all over his face*. He has two eyes – small and round – two ears – big and floppy, *FOUR* legs and *NO* arms. No wonder he's useless on a keyboard. He has ginger eyebrows but the rest of him is splotchy brown. His tail – I think it's a tail – is short and stubby. Perhaps he caught it in a door. I just didn't know what to make of Hector, and I could see he felt the same about me.

Tipperary smiled when she saw I had my eyes open. "You look hungry," she said. "I'll fry you an egg."

Fried egg is terrible. You couldn't eat one without any teeth even if you wanted to – which I didn't. I spat it out as fast as Tipperary fed it to me.

"Kind of a messy eater, aren't you?" she said. "Never mind. Let's try something else."

She heated up some milk and fed me sips. It felt nice, holding the warm milk in my mouth and letting it dribble down my chin. When I'd finished, she tore a towel in half and tied it round my bottom. It felt ridiculous. When she picked me up, it fell off. She put it back on and knotted it.

"I've never put a nappy on before," she said. "It's harder than it looks. But this should catch

11

the worst of it."

The worst of what, I wondered? I was a bit surprised when I found out. Where I come from, we don't do that.

Tipperary fed me more sips of warm milk and I began to sink into a soft, deep sleep. I'd come a long way and I was tired. The last thing I saw before I nodded off was Hector's round brown eyes fixed on me jealously.

These Earth people are weird, I thought. I didn't know that Hector was a dog.

3 Holy Moley

Next morning Tipperary fed me *more* warm milk. She gave Hector a whole packet of biscuits and he wolfed the lot. Then he ran outside. He balanced on three legs and did something peculiar. That's funny, I thought, Hector's raining. I hadn't quite got Earth talk sorted out – they told me before I left home that it would take a while.

When I'd finished my milk, Tipperary propped me up and patted my back. After a while I felt a bubble rise up from my stomach. My mouth flew open and the bubble shot out with a croaking noise.

"Nice one," she said, and patted me some more. I made several more bubbles. Some went up and some went down. Then it was time to have my nappy changed.

"Holy Moley!" Tipperary said, when she'd got the old nappy off. "Where does all this stuff come from?"

I didn't say anything – I didn't know either. Hector watched with a superior look on his face.

"Don't you have a grown-up?" Tipperary asked while she cleaned me up. "Like a mum? Or a dad? Or somebody?"

I didn't answer.

"Maybe you lost 'em eh? Or maybe they lost you. Maybe your nappies were too much for 'em. You're kind of nice though – don't you think, Hector?"

"No," growled Hector. **"Notnice. Notnotnot nicebaby!"**

"Suit yourself, Hector. In any case we'll take him down the mountain when the rain stops. We'll hand him over to the police."

Hector perked up right away.

Rain was drumming on the tent, making me think of huge three-legged dogs. I snuggled down inside Tipperary's jacket, shut my eyes

14

and slept. I slept until Hector shoved his cold nose into my warm belly.

"**She'smine**," he growled. Dog is a gruff and growly language. "**Notyours. Don'tyouforgetit.**"

"Yours?" I asked. "Is she your mother? You don't take after her."

"**Notmotherstupid!**" he growled. "**I'madog she'sTippperaryandyou'restupid!**"

"Not compared to you," I said. "I've scanned your brain. It's nothing to write home about."

"**Forsomebodywhogotleftunderarockyou've gotabighead**," he snapped. Dogs can be very personal.

"It does feel big," I agreed. "And sort of wobbly. Must be all that brain inside it. Which is one problem you don't have."

Hector got up and stalked out of the tent. He stalked back in immediately and shook himself all over me and Tipperary.

"Rainingcatsanddogs!" he said.

I thought that sounded interesting but when I looked out all I could see was water. Hector obviously tells fibs.

Tipperary sat up and wiped her face. "Hector!" she said. "Don't shake on me! You've woken the nappy monster and he's hungry again. D'you think he likes mashed banana?"

Hector woofed in a *don'tknowdon'tcare* way and chased a flea over his shoulder and down his leg.

I smiled and pulled Tipperary's orange hair and ate my mashed banana. It was quite nice, but rather... well... *mashed.*

Where I come from, we take our nourishment by photosynthesis. We use energy from sunlight to produce food from gas and water. You have to be green to do it, but at least you don't get bits stuck to your face.

I ate up all the banana and Tipperary used up all the bits of towel for nappies before midday.

I'm not sure, but I think there's a connection there.

4 Everything Sticks Together

"Come on, let's take the nappy monster down the mountain, Hector," Tipperary said when the rain stopped. It was midday, the sun was shining and the ground was steaming.

"**Yes! Yes!! Yes!!!**" barked Hector. Hector likes to *go* – he doesn't mind where. Also, he just couldn't wait to get rid of me.

"Better do one last clean-up job on the little shebango before we hand him over to Lost Property," Tipperary sighed, shaking her head and ripping up a T-shirt. She held both my feet in one hand to keep them out of the way while she dabbed at me. She blew a raspberry on my

17

fat clean bottom. I thought, *it's now or never.*

"Hey," I said. "Stop it. That noise tickles."

Tipperary dropped my feet and rubbed her hands across her face. She didn't look at me. She looked at Hector.

"Hector – is my brain on the wane?" she asked. "Because I thought the little egg-head spoke."

"I *did*," I said. "If Hector can talk, why shouldn't I?"

"Hector can't. Hector is a razzle-dazzle dog but he can't *talk*."

"Cancan*cancan!*" Hector yapped. All Tipperary heard was "Rufrruffrrrufff*rrrrufffff!*"

"Not English, anyway," Tipperary said, patting his head. "He speaks very good dog."

"Verygooddog!Veryverygood*dog!*Veryvery verygood*dog!*Dogbasketsdogbasketsdog **baskets!**" Hector yelped, bouncing up and down on all four paws at once. This is not a good thing for a big dog to do inside a small tent.

"Tell him to shut up and listen, Tipperary," I said, when she'd finished untangling him from her backpack.

Hector sat down and sulked.

"OK," said Tipperary, stroking the fluff that grew on my head. "I'll pretend that you're a talking baby. Why not? What's your name?"

"I haven't got one yet. Back home I'm not old enough for that. I'm only in my first decade. We don't get named until at least our third. I was meant to be older than this when I got here. Somebody on my planet can't count."

Tipperary's round eyes got rounder suddenly. "Somebody on your *planet*? Are you telling me you're a talking baby from outer *space*?"

"That's right. I've come to fix a fault in gravity – Earth's gravity, that is. What did you do with my computer?"

"What computer, egg-head?"

"There should have been one with me when you found me."

"It was pitch dark and raining stair rods – I only just found *you*. What did it look like?"

"White and sort of oblong. Kind of round at both ends. State of the art."

Hector looked guilty.

"Hector... you *didn't*?" Tipperary asked.

"*Bad dog!*"

"Lookedlikeabone," Hector replied. "Tasted awful."

19

Tipperary couldn't understand him – she doesn't speak dog. But I could.

"You idiot!" I said. "You ate my computer!"

Hector began to growl. I growled back.

"Cool it, you two!" Tipperary snapped.

"I'd like a name please, Tipperary," I said, when Hector had shut up. "You both have them, I want one too. A good one – like yours."

"Mine's for a girl. You need one for a boy."

"Do I?" I asked. "How do you know?"

"I should do. I've changed your nappy enough times."

"What's that got to do with it?"

Tipperary shook her head. "Never mind, moonshine," she said. "How about Moses? Moses was found in a river. If Hector hadn't found you when he did, you'd have been in one too."

"Moses sounds good," I said. "I like Moses."

"So what's this gravity business, Moses?"

"Well," I began. "You know what gravity does, don't you?" I asked them both.

"Neverheardofit," Hector growled. **"Gravyyes. Gravityno."**

"It's what makes things fall down instead of up – right?" Tipperary said.

"Right. Gravity pulls everything towards the middle," I explained.

"Middleofwhat?" asked Hector.

"Anything, dog brain."

Tipperary sighed. "Don't bark, Moses. It makes me jump."

"I'm talking to Hector."

"Does he understand you?"

"Not when I'm talking gravity. Listen, Hector. Gravity is what pulls everything in towards everything else. OK?"

"Ifyousaysowobblehead."

"It wasn't *me* that said so, Hector. It was Sir Isaac Newton. In 1685."

"Hey! Let me in on the gravity situation, Moses!" Tipperary said.

"I was telling Hector about Sir Isaac Newton. He discovered the Binomial Theorem. And the Differential and Integral Calculus. You know, *every particle of matter in the universe attracts every other particle...* You *must* have read his Universal Law of Gravitation, Tipperary. Of course, Albert Einstein carried on where Isaac Newton left off."

"Of *course.*"

"It just means everything sticks together.

Which reminds me. Would you mind changing my nappy before I go on?"

"*Didgeridoo!*" she said, when she'd got the old one off. "If people were buying this stuff, we'd be rich!"

"So," I explained, when I was comfy again. "Gravity is what makes everything stick to the Earth. Even though the Earth is round, like a conker. Instead of falling off."

"Into space, you mean?"

"That's right. Into space."

Hector got up, yawned in a show-off kind of way, and did that thing dogs do when one of their legs starts to work all on its own – like a wind-up toy – and they can scratch behind their ear so fast it looks as though they're scratching with eight legs. I could see that Isaac Newton's law of gravitation was news to him.

"But here on Earth it isn't working properly," I said, ignoring Hector. "It's gone wrong."

"You mean – stuff is going to start floating about, Moses? Falling off? Into space?"

"Not just stuff, Tipperary. *Us. We are going to start falling off.*"

5 SOFTIE

Tipperary picked me up and held me to her chest, squashing my nose. "You're saying we could die," she said quietly. She looked up at the mountain. "Everything could die." She held me tighter. "Don't cry, Moses. I won't let you fall off into space."

"I'm not crying," I said. "I'm dribbling. It's because I can't breathe through my nose."

I struggled to turn my head sideways so that my cheek was pressed against her shoulder and my nose could unblock. In this position I could only look down. I was forced to stare straight into Hector's eyes. He stared straight back in a scornful kind of way.

"Dying is not so bad," I said. "You just turn into something else. Smoke. Leaves. Frost. Whatever."

"Bones," said Hector.

"Could you put me down, Tipperary? I want to concentrate. I'm going to need a telephone and I'll have to borrow a computer. Some dog brain's eaten mine."

Hector glowered.

"No problem," Tipperary said. "I've got everything you need on **SOFTIE** – that's my bus. Let's get down the mountain."

She clapped an old hat on her head and stuffed her clothes and sleeping bag into her backpack. She took down the tent, rolled it up, and tied it on top. Her pot, pan, plate, knife, fork, spoon, mug and tiny stove dangled underneath. She looked like an elongated turtle once she'd heaved the pack up on to her shoulders, and she clanked like a knight in armour. But she had both arms free for carrying me.

Hector didn't carry anything. He just got in the way. Even so, it only took about an hour to get down off Mount Wrath – Tipperary's fast on her feet.

I was impressed when I saw **SOFTIE**. That bus was a work of art. Each passenger station had its own computer with CD-ROM and modem. There was a video conferencing facility so you could talk to several different people on the phone and see them all at the same time. There were books, comics, magazines, annuals and toys.

Earth babies seem to have a lot of things to suck and chew that are not food. You can't eat them – I tried. They also have small stuffed creatures covered in fur. So, I thought – rabbits are pink down here, just like they are at home.

There was TV too, but Earth TV is funny – there are hardly any programmes about other planets and most of them are crazy. Earth people think Earth is the only planet in the universe where anybody lives. The best bits of Earth TV tell you what to buy, the rest is pretty boring.

There were reclining seats, hammocks and beanbags. Hector had a Comfy Dog-Eze basket with his own personal flea trap and biscuit dispenser. None of it was quite as comfortable as what we have at home – you can't beat sleeping in warm jelly can you? – but it wasn't bad.

S O F

There was a snack bar in the back of the bus and power showers for tired travellers. In the middle of the bus there was a soft play-space where you could roll about and fall off things without getting hurt. I found that useful.

Tipperary said she would let people ride on her bus just for fun, whether they needed to go anywhere or not. Tired mothers with teething babies would jump on **SOFTIE** just for a rest. Teething is another of those things I didn't know about when I arrived. If Earth babies need teeth, why aren't they born with them?

Tipperary designed and built **SOFTIE** herself. Her mother was the chief engineer on a container ship and she taught Tipperary how to build an engine. Her father was a panel beater and he helped her with the chassis. They made a lovely job of it. Streamlined, like a sucked fruit drop.

Tipperary sat me down with a stack of books and a few CDs to help me learn about Earth. The first thing I had to understand was *time*.

Dad said I've got three days to put things right down here. He's coming back for me on Saturday night. That's all very well – at least it would be – but whoever organised my trip made a mistake. I was *definitely* meant to be older than this when I got here. Still, I reckon I'm developing pretty fast. I wonder how soon I'll be out of nappies? As far as I can tell, time is different for different creatures here. Some things are born, grow up, grow old and die all in one day. Others take many hundred years. There are evidently several different kinds of time working at once.

Tipperary lives on board the bus. **SOFTIE**'s her home. "Hector and me don't like houses," she said. "We like to move – but we have our favourite stopping places. Our best is quite near here – with my Aunt Doris. That's where I'm going to take you."

Tipperary hadn't seen Aunt Doris for a while. She gave us a warm welcome, especially me. Hector gave Aunt Doris's hens quite a warm welcome too, till he remembered that he wasn't allowed to chase them.

"My hens are sensitive creatures, Hector," Aunt Doris scolded. "Easily upset. You be civil to them."

She picked me up and cuddled me. "Congratulations, dear," she said to Tipperary.

"You never said you were expecting."

"That's because I wasn't – he's not mine, Aunt Doris!" Tipperary said. "I *found* him on the mountain! Well, Hector found him really."

Aunt Doris gave Tipperary a funny look. "I don't care where he came from, dear, you've got a proper treasure there. One to be proud of. You make yourselves comfortable in my field, and I hope you'll both be very happy."

We would have been, if we'd had time.

There was a little spinney by Aunt Doris's field and Tipperary parked the bus beside it. The place was so beautiful it took my breath away. Trees don't say much but they feel like family to me.

6 Hole at the Pole

Thursday was Aunt Doris's afternoon for whist in the village hall, so once she'd settled us into the spinney, Tipperary, Hector and I were on our own for an hour or two.

I had quite a bit to do and not much time to do it in. I began by explaining my plans to Tipperary. I soon found out she was no expert when it came to physics – and Hector hadn't got a clue.

Physics is what we start with at school but Hector says dogs don't even go to school on Earth. I can't understand that. At home dogs always get the best marks.

Anyway, Tipperary made me comfortable on a beanbag. She settled herself into a hammock and started polishing a bit of engine. You never see Tipperary without a rag in her hand and oil on her face. It suits her, really.

Hector curled up on a beanbag beside me, and I did my best to make them both understand the gravity situation and exactly what I planned to do about it. Well, to make Tipperary understand. Hector didn't seem to *want* to understand.

"Remember what I said about gravity, up on the mountain?" I began.

"Notgravyagain," Hector said.

"You said we're going to float off into space," Tipperary nodded, spitting on her rag. "But you didn't say *why* and you didn't say *when*."

"*Why* doesn't matter. The Earth is getting lighter, that's all. That means gravity can't suck so hard. *When* is not much more than forty-eight hours away. The effects will start slowly and build up."

"But *why's* it getting lighter, Moses? It should be getting heavier. There are 10,000 new babies being born every hour just for a start. Holy Moley, that's a lot of nappies!"

Hector made an **"oh-yuk"** face.

"Listen," I said. "You know the middle of this planet is all hot and runny?"

"Likeyournappies," Hector said.

I ignored him. "Well, there's a hole at the North Pole and the molten magma has started to leak. It's turning into gas and blowing away."

Hector chuckled.

"How did that happen, Moses?"

I felt my face going red. "It was an accident," I said.

"It must have been a big one."

"I didn't *mean* to do it."

"You did it, Moses? *You* made a hole in the North Pole? HOW???"

"I was only doing my homework. I had to get to level three on my computer game."

"You messed up Earth's gravity with a computer game? On another planet? **HOW?**"

"I told you. Playing CYBERFLOAT. Mum said I could send a note down saying sorry. Dad said that wasn't good enough. He said – '*You broke it, sunshine, you can fix it.*'"

"Quite right," said Tipperary. "I agree with your dad. And playing on a computer isn't homework. It's mucking about."

"Didn't you ever muck about at school, Tipperary?"

Tipperary went red and looked out of the window.

"Well... sometimes," she said. "Maybe."

"Only sometimes? Lucky you. We have to muck about all day. We get absolutely sick of it. *'Put that book down,'* the teachers say if they catch us reading. *'You're not here to read. You're here to muck about. Get back on your computer* **at once!***"

Tipperary shook her head and went on polishing. "Explain," she said. "About the hole in the Pole."

"Have you ever played CYBERFLOAT?" I asked.

Tipperary shook her head again.

"It's great. All you need is a computer and a grasp of the quantum theory. But here's the spooky part. The whole point of CYBERFLOAT is that *you're stranded on a planet where gravity's gone wrong!*"

Hector stuck his head under his beanbag.

"Go on," said Tipperary.

"First you choose your gravity malfunction. You can have:

Heavy Moon, Rubbish Dump, or Slow Down."

Hector picked up his beanbag in his teeth, and carried it to the far end of the bus.

"Don't mind Hector," Tipperary said. "You carry on."

"**Heavy Moon** is where giant electric eels are invading the Sea of Tranquillity. They make the moon so heavy that its gravity gets strong enough to suck things – ships, mountains, whales, anything – off all the neighbouring planets. You have to catch the things and put them back on the planets and catch the eels and drop them down black holes. There are three levels and each time you move up one, the eels get bigger and the black holes get smaller. Oh, and the holes move about. And so do the eels."

"Sounds great," Tipperary said.

"**Rubbish Dump** is where people have dumped stuff in space – old space rockets, factories, moon buggies, crisp wrappers, crocodiles, leaky roofs, steam trains, space stations. Any old thing. You have to pick up the junk and drop it back down where it came from. Each time you move up a level, the rubbish moves faster.

"What about **Slow Down**?"

"**Slow Down** is where the planet is spinning too slowly. That weakens gravity, so you have to flick the planet on to a piece of string stretched between two sticks and make it run up and down the string so it spins faster and faster. When you've got it going fast enough, you flip it off the string and back into orbit. But it has to be the right orbit, otherwise you get inter-planetary collisions all over the galaxy."

Tipperary nodded. "So tell me, Moses – how exactly did you put a hole in the Pole playing CYBERFLOAT?"

"It's a mystery. Even my dad can't understand it. We think it happened when I zapped an electric eel on level three of

Heavy Moon. Somehow it zapped right back. The double zap blasted off and zapped all the way to Earth and landed at the North Pole. Dad says it's all my fault – but I know how to fix it."

"How?"

"All I have to do is find a way to generate an electromagnetic wave powerful enough to reverse the polarity of the electrical charge in the molten magma."

"That simple, huh?"

"Then the magma will be sucked back into the middle of the Earth and everything will be back to normal."

"Piece of cake," said Tipperary. "How are you going to do it?"

"I think I can make the wave the way I made the zap – with a computer game. I like computer games. I play them a lot. I don't want to boast but I'm known on the internets of three solar systems as the Ace from Space."

Hector yawned.

"I'll need a few top players here on Earth. What's the quickest way to find them?"

"Try the internet," Tipperary said.

I nodded. "I want about six players, all

playing at once – like an orchestra. I'll be like their conductor. If they all finish the same game at the same time, I reckon they could generate enough zap to set off the kind of electromagnetic wave I need. But we've got to do it by midnight on Saturday. Dad says if I'm not ready he'll go without me. Anyway, if I haven't fixed things by then, the magma will all be gone."

"What happens when the magma's all gone?"

"The Earth crumples up."

"Whattt???!!!"

"Stay cool, Tipperary. It's not going to happen. I'll fix it."

"SobuckupEinstein," Hector snapped.

"I would. But some dog brain has eaten my computer."

7 Squidgum Didgum

That evening, Aunt Doris cooked mushroom stew for supper. It smelled really good, but I didn't get much and what I did get was all mashed up. I had just decided that I definitely prefer photosynthesis, when Aunt Doris winked at Tipperary and popped a teaspoonful of something freezing cold into my mouth.

"What d'you make of mint-choc-chip, egg-head?" Tipperary asked.

It was wonderful. I could have eaten loads of it, but all I got was one measly eggcupful because Aunt Doris said it was bad for my teeth. I don't understand. I haven't got any teeth.

I spent Thursday night cuddled up with
Tipperary in a saggy brass bed in Aunt Doris's
spare room. Every time Tipperary turned over,
her boots, which she'd hung over the bed knob,
banged together and woke me up. I was
beginning to miss my mother. I missed my
father too, even though it was his fault that I was
here. Sort of. Anyway, it was nice to feel
Tipperary's arm round me and hear her snoring
in my ear.

One time when I woke up she wasn't there
any more. She was sitting on the end of the bed
blowing down a tube. She was making a weird
noise – it reminded me of home and trees and
firelight and friends talking.

"That's nice," I said. "What is it?"

"Didgeridoo," she said, and went on blowing.

In the morning, Aunt Doris asked Tipperary to
collect the eggs. "Friday's Egg Day, dear," she
said, "and my Egg Ladies will be along any
minute."

"Before we get busy, Aunt Doris, I've got
something to tell you," Tipperary said. "It's
about Moses."

"If you've got things you want to tell your

auntie, you tell 'em, my dear," Aunt Doris said. "But you'll have to wait until the Egg Ladies have been."

Tipperary stomped off to look for eggs. Aunt Doris's hens lay them anywhere. Behind bales of straw. In clumps of nettles. Under the hedge. I was looking forward to seeing the Egg Ladies, but when the first one came into the yard I found out she was just an ordinary person who had come to buy eggs!

The Egg Ladies were mad about me. Some of them spoke a most peculiar language. *"Give your auntie a kiss, my little opsy-popsy poppet! Who's got little squidgum-didgum chubby dubby cheeks then? Who's a little oochy-coochy cuddles?"*

I wouldn't have minded, but Hector kept laughing.

They were a friendly crowd, fond of Aunt Doris and always glad to see Tipperary. One person in the yard was different though. He had glinty grey eyes and a horrible smile – all teeth. Just looking at him gave me the shivers. He hadn't come to buy eggs. He wasn't friendly. And he certainly wasn't glad to see Tipperary.

"That's Silas Stoatwarden," Aunt Doris

whispered when she saw him coming through the gate. "He lives up at the big house. Studies flying saucers. I wonder what he wants?"

We soon found out.

"Who gave you permission to park that eyesore in the spinney?" he snarled at Tipperary, pointing at **SOFTIE** with a long, thin finger.

"Who gave you permission to ask?" Tipperary snapped back, rubbing at a damp patch I'd left on her shoulder.

"Well you can't stop here," Stoatwarden said. "There's a law against it."

"That's my bus you're talking about," Tipperary told him. "And it's parked in my aunt's spinney."

"I don't care whose bus it is. Or whose spinney. This is a respectable neighbourhood and I for one won't have it overrun with riffraff in buses! Not them, not their babies, and not their mangy dogs!"

Hector began to rumble. Silas Stoatwarden picked up a stick.

"My niece is as good as anyone, Silas Stoatwarden," Aunt Doris said, hopping between them. "*Better*, most likely. So is that baby. And so is the dog. Put that stick down before Hector hurts you, and get off my land."

"Animals like that one ought to be destroyed," said Silas Stoatwarden. "I shouldn't be surprised if something happened to that animal some dark night. Riffraff. The world is full of riffraff."

He glanced at Tipperary scornfully as he was leaving. He noticed me, stopped, looked and looked again. He gave a piercing stare, deep into my eyes. "Nice little riffraff," he said. "Can I hold him?"

Tipperary shook her head.

"Just for a minute," Silas Stoatwarden wheedled.

"No chance," Tipperary snapped. "Get lost!"

Silas Stoatwarden glared at me. "Is that your child?" he asked Tipperary.

Tipperary nodded but I don't think Silas Stoatwarden believed her. I had a horrible feeling that somehow he'd guessed who I was and where I'd come from. I began to cry.

The hair on Hector's neck went all bristly. He pulled his lips back off his teeth and growled. Silas Stoatwarden shrugged and walked slowly out of the yard.

"That's him gone, and good riddance!" Aunt Doris said.

Somehow I didn't think it was.

I was right. We hadn't seen the last of Silas Stoatwarden.

I began to feel a little desperate. I had a nasty feeling that Stoatwarden knew I was an alien. But Aunt Doris still didn't. And I badly needed to start work on the internet. Time was passing fast – it was Friday lunch time already – and I was getting nowhere.

"Come on," I whispered to Tipperary. "Let's get started on the bus."

"I've got to explain to Aunt Doris about you and gravity first," she said. "I want to break it to her gently. She's not as young as she was. I'll do it as soon as she's counted the egg money."

As it turned out, Aunt Doris overheard me talking to Bess, her prize Buff Orpington hen, before Tipperary got a chance to tell her anything. I was talking chicken, naturally, but Aunt Doris understood at once that we were in communication.

Bess was telling me where I could find some particularly juicy caterpillars. I was trying to make her understand that I don't eat

46

caterpillars. Hens aren't good at seeing other people's points of view. She kept insisting on how succulent they were – with a hint of pepper to them – because they'd been feeding on cress by the pond.

I kept saying, "Yes, yes, I bet they're lovely, but I don't eat them."

Tipperary had left me in a basket hanging from the apple tree, out of harm's way, while she took the egg money indoors. Bess was perched close by. Suddenly, I looked up and there was Aunt Doris, watching me and Bess with her beady brown eye – not unlike a hen's eye, but more friendly.

"Tipperary!" she screeched. "Tipperary! Come out here quick! Your boy Moses is squawking like a chicken! I do believe he's talking to my Bess!"

Tipperary ran up and lifted me out of my basket. She sat down under the apple tree and balanced me on her knees.

"You sit down too, Aunt Doris," she said.

"Don't speak to me as if you think I'm queer in the head, girl," Aunt Doris said. "Because I'm not."

"I know you're not, Aunt Doris. Moses *can*

talk. He talks to me. He talks to Hector. It's no surprise to me if he can talk to Bess. He could probably talk to an egg."

"Well, I've tried, Tipperary," I interrupted. "But they don't have anything to say unless they're just about to hatch, and then it's only '*Help!*' or '*Get me out of here!*'"

Aunt Doris sat perfectly still. She didn't look at me or Tipperary. She watched Bess fly down to scratch in the earth under the apple tree. Tipperary took Aunt Doris's brown hand and held it.

"I should have told you before," she said. She told Aunt Doris all about how Hector found me on Mount Wrath. Then I told her all about gravity and the North Pole and how I only had till Saturday night to fix it.

Aunt Doris listened. Then she picked me up and had a good look at me. "I don't care where you came from, son," she said. "You're welcome here." She kissed me and gave me back to Tipperary. "I never did trust computers," she added. Then she went indoors and made a pot of tea.

Tipperary smiled, and filled my bottle with Aunt Doris's home-made dandelion and burdock. It's delicious, but I only got a drop.

"You may have the brain of an Einstein, Moses," Aunt Doris said when I asked for more, "but you have the digestive system of an ordinary baby and it's our job to keep you regular."

Tipperary sat me on her lap and held the bottle for me while I drank. I leaned back against her and began to calculate the precise power of the electromagnetic wave I was going to need. It was going to take a big one. I had no idea if my plan would work.

8 Oh, Blissful Sky

Hector was asleep under Aunt Doris's porch. He's not an active sort of dog and afternoons are his quiet time. Aunt Doris said that I looked sleepy too.

"I'm not," I said, although I was. "I want to go on the computer."

"Don't argue," Aunt Doris said. "I know a sleepy baby when I see one. Put him down for a nap, Tipperary. He can save the planet after he's had his beauty sleep."

Tipperary looked at me and shrugged. "It doesn't pay to disobey," she said. "Not where Aunt Doris is concerned." She carried me over to the bus and laid me down on a beanbag.

She tiptoed outside to Aunt Doris and they sat in the field with a bottle of some kind of drink. There were flowers floating in it. They kept tasting it, and adding things, and tasting it again. Before long, Aunt Doris was asking Tipperary riddles about chickens and Tipperary was lying on her back in the grass with her boots in the air.

Presently Aunt Doris said she was going indoors for a nap. "We're in for a busy night with young Moses and his electromagnetic whatnot," she said, "and I feel like a feather on the float! I could do with a doze."

"Me too," smiled Tipperary, kicking off her boots. "I could use a snooze."

All of a sudden, Aunt Doris turned chalk white and pointed at the sky. Tipperary put up her hand to shade her eyes and stared upwards. I craned my head round on the beanbag until I could see what they were looking at.

It was a golden blur of feathers, high in the sky, soaring, dipping, diving, floating, riding higher and higher on the upcurrents of autumn sunshine, clucking and squawking in aeroballetic joy.

It was Bess. I could see her and hear her from down on my beanbag.

"Oh joy!" she cackled. "Oh glory! Oh blissful, blissful sky! This is what I was hatched for! Come on up, girls! Spread those chicken wings and soar!"

The other hens gazed up at her, first with disapproval, then with jealousy, then with uncontainable excitement. One after another they launched themselves cackling skywards. Soon the whole flock were spiralling up into the heavens, which are the rightful home of all birds, even chickens.

Aunt Doris shook her head. "That elderflower wine is a powerful brew," she said. "I could swear that was old Bess soaring like an eagle aloft."

"It is," Tipperary whispered. "They all are."

"They're hens," Aunt Doris said. "Hens don't *soar*. Some of mine can't hardly hop up on to their perches of a night time. I have to lift old Bess when her arthritis gives her jip."

"They're soaring now, Aunt Doris."

"Can't be, girl. 'Tis the wine. We'd best have our forty winks. Where's the baby?"

"He's in the bus, Aunt Doris. Safe as houses. If houses are safe. Me, I prefer buses."

Aunt Doris staggered indoors, still shaking her head. Tipperary rolled up her jacket, tucked it under her head and began to snore.

9 Mousemousemousemouse

I was still lying on my beanbag in the bus, feeling uncomfortable. I had wind, and my feet kept floating up. I lay with my feet in the air and looked out of the window. Every now and then Bess would whiz past like a rocket.

I felt sort of bloated, because of the wind, and my eyes kept crossing. I needed to concentrate on gravity but it's hard to do that with a stomach ache. There's only one thing to do about wind and that's get rid of it. There are two ways of doing that.

I tried burping but that didn't work. I tried the other way and that did. The back-blast lifted me gently into the air, where I hovered, suspended above the beanbag like a small striped cloud.

I knew at once what was going on. It was gravity. Or rather, it wasn't. I drifted down towards the TV at the back of the bus. It took me some time to grab the remote and switch it on. When I did, there were news flashes on all channels. It had started. I caught a special News Flash from News Round. A man called Charley Cool was talking. He was wildly excited.

"This is incredible!" he cried. "This is so cool! Children everywhere have started bouncing! Schools are going crazy!"

The camera showed us what was going on. Small books, about the size of this one, floated out of book boxes and hovered untidily about classrooms. Worksheets were getting stuck to ceilings. Displays of work that had taken all morning to pin up tugged themselves loose from walls and flapped up stairwells like flocks of large, flat parrots.

The camera moved into a dining hall.

"Dinner ladies demand danger money because of flying cutlery!" Charley Cool announced.

Nets were strung hurriedly over school

playgrounds
to stop the smallest
children from bouncing over
playground walls and floating away.
Drinks poured up people's noses. Toilets
flooded. Children loved it. Grown-ups grumbled.
Hairstyles went wild. Washing hung up, not
down. The number of apples to the kilo
quadrupled and Weight Watchers announced
incredible success stories.

Nobody except me had a
clue about the danger that
was threatening Earth.

Hovering above the
television screen, blown
this way and that by my
own noisy digestive system,
I finally managed to hit the

right keys and switch on a computer. I needed some time in cyberspace – urgently. Perhaps I should have called for Tipperary to come and help me – but she was sound asleep.

I was getting nowhere fast, when Hector came bouncing up the steps on to the bus. **"Badbaby!"** he barked, rudely. **"Badbadbaby!!"**

I dropped the remote and accidentally switched everything back off. "I am not a bad baby, you idiot. And you just made me drop the remote."

"WhatyoutouchingTipperary'sstufffor?"

"I'm *trying* to save the planet, Hector."

"FatchanceWobblehead!Youcan'tevencatch fleasyet!"

"I haven't *got* fleas, Hector. Unlike you. Do you *want* me to correct the fault in the gravitational constant? Or not?"

Hector raised one eyebrow, which is how dogs shrug.

"Don'tcare," he snapped. He was about to hop off down the steps and out into the field, when I decided to try begging.

"Hector," I wheedled. *"Please* help. I *need* your help." It was true. I did.

Hector turned round and came trotting back.

His heart is in the right place. It's only his brain that malfunctions.

"I need you to launch me into cyberspace, Hector," I said. Hector looked blank. He doesn't have a clue what cyberspace is. "I've got to get on to the internet," I explained. "I'll tell you what to do. Use the mouse, Hector. Click with your paw when I tell you."

All Hector had to do was get the cursor to the icon and click. He might have managed it, if he hadn't got so overexcited when I said *mouse*.

"Wheremouse?" he growled. **"Mouse mousemousemouse!Snipsnapmousebe gonewhenHectorfindit!"**

In the end he got the cursor into position and clicked. Getting him to type in the right series of letters to get us on to the internet took patience. Hector doesn't know his alphabet and he can't count past three. He wouldn't understand the internet if it landed on his head.

"Hit *Control K*, Hector," I barked. "Control is the bottom one, on the toybox side. Good. Now hold it down, and use your other paw to hit *K*! *K*!! Second from bottom row, Hector. Five along from the window side. *Five!* NO, Hector. That's *L*. And that's *J*. The one in the *middle*! YES!!! Oh,

Hector. You let Control go. Start again."

"**Won't,**" said Hector. "**Shan't.**"

"Oh well," I sighed. "At least switch on the TV so I can see what's happening in the world. Push the button, Hector. Use your paw."

Hector did, and the set flicked on. Charley Cool was gone and in his place four Top Experts were discussing gravity. Each one had their own ideas about what had gone wrong with it and why. None of them had noticed the hole at the North Pole.

The first one said that aliens were behind the problem. Not far wrong really.

The second one said it was all down to foreigners interfering with the weather. Right again, in a way.

The third one thought giant tree frogs were invading the galaxy.

The fourth one was Silas Stoatwarden. Apparently he's an expert on astrodynamics. He said it was high time people learned to keep both feet on the ground, especially young people and dogs. He said a good dose of old-fashioned discipline would sort the whole thing out. He said he had a good idea of who was at the bottom of it all and that he'd be taking action shortly. That worried me.

"Switch off, Hector, I've seen enough," I said. Hector pressed the button with his paw and the set clicked off.

"Here's what we'll do," I said. "We'll take it step by step. First, I'll tell you exactly how to get me on the net."

Hector was slow, even for a dog, but we were finally beginning to make some progress, when he hit the wrong key for the third time running and messed everything up.

10 Dog Breath

I called Hector *Dog Breath*. He called me *Wobblehead*. I pulled his whiskers. He stuck his nose underneath me and shoved. And I went flying. Literally.

I whizzed down the aisle, bounced off the top step, missed the second and landed on top of poor old Bess, who had finally stopped looping the loop and was on her way back from the pond, bursting with caterpillars.

Bess shot into the air squawking, and came down on top of Tipperary, feathers flying, beak wide open, screeching like a banshee.

"Help! Help! Wake up, Tipperary! The sky's

falling down!"

Tipperary woke up, and jumped up, and scooped me up into her arms all in one jet-propelled second.

Once she knew I was all right she said some very rude words. She said Bess was a pea-brained chicken and Hector was a useless mutt. She said I was nothing but an interfering baby. She said she'd been doing just fine until I dropped in from outer space and messed up her life. Then she burst into tears and told Aunt Doris that she – meaning herself – didn't deserve me and that the worst person in the world would look after me better than she did.

Aunt Doris sat her down on the sofa with me in her arms and gave us both a hug.

"Listen to me, my girl," she said. "You're a Top Class Mother to that baby. Top Class. There isn't a baby in the world that hasn't had a narrow escape. You had several yourself. I well remember the time you fell out of your cot and got stuck upside-down in the ship's laundry basket. Your mother and I searched all over for you. Your mother thought you'd fallen overboard and drowned – just about broke her heart. We couldn't hear you hollering, 'cos you was all muffled up in last week's washing. In the end, we saw your little boots a-waving. Life is a dangerous business, Tipperary. That's it and all about it. So dry your eyes and I'll make us all a batch of scones."

Aunt Doris made the scones. Tipperary gave Bess a whole one to herself for breaking my fall, and Hector a whole one to make him feel useful again, even though it was his fault I fell on Bess. All I got was a mouthful of mashed-up crumbs.

When everyone had settled down, I told them the gravity business had started. "You might not have noticed yet because you've been asleep," I said. "But you will now. Stand up and jump, Aunt Doris."

Aunt Doris jumped. She rose slowly into the air and floated up towards the ceiling.

"Push off!" I shouted.

"I *beg* your pardon, Moses!"

"Push off from the rafters, before you hit the ceiling!"

Aunt Doris did. She drifted back down to the floor and sat down all of a tremble.

Tipperary passed me to Aunt Doris. She flapped her arms, and rose smoothly up to the ceiling. She blew a noisy raspberry at the roof beams and sank gracefully back down towards the floor. On the way down she stopped and turned a somersault.

Hector barked ecstatically. He loves a bit of excitement.

Tipperary stopped smiling. She held tightly to Aunt Doris, who held tightly to me. "Do you know what this means?" she asked.

Aunt Doris nodded. "It means the end of everything," she said. "Unless young Moses here can put things right."

Nobody spoke. Everyone was silent. Even Hector.

11 ICARUS

Tipperary tied a large encyclopedia to the toe of my babygrow just in case, and a bag of sugar to Hector's collar. She filled hers and Aunt Doris's pockets with marbles and we went out to the bus. Aunt Doris loaded sacks of sand and cement from her barn into a wheelbarrow, and Tipperary heaved them on to the bus for ballast. Then we got to work.

I was on the net in no time. Soon I was talking to the members of **ICARUS**, or the Inter-Continental **A**ll **R**ound **U**nbeatable **S**tars:

      Irina from **Moscow,**
      Mitch from **Chicago,**

Grace Miliswa from **Johannesburg,**
Ajaz from **London,**
Zik from **Lagos,**
and **Sachiko** from **Kyoto.**

There must be an inter-galactic web site somewhere on the net, one that's known only to children, because ICARUS had heard of me. They were surprised to find the Ace from Space was only a baby, but when I told them what I wanted them to do and why, they agreed to cooperate.

Zucchini was their favourite computer game.

"It's about a planet called Zygophyllaceous," Zik explained. "*Zucchini* for short. There are three parts to the game and each part has three levels. You start with Spinner Dinner. That's where giant spiders are invading space and winding their long hairy legs round Zucchini, gobbling up the little Succhinoids like greenfly. The sound effects are great. You can spray the spiders with Superdestructo, but that wipes out the planet and finishes the game. Or you can tempt them away from Zucchini by laying a trail of juicy bluebottles across the galaxy."

"Yum yum."

"Shark Attack comes after Spinner Dinner. Mutant sharks come out of the oceans and chomp up everybody on the land. They swim up rivers and lurk in ponds and jump out at you. Some of them even come up drains and squeeze through plugholes into your bath. You have to catch them in a net, before they catch you, and drop them back into Shark Ocean."

"Then what?"

"Then comes Zap Trap. Giant tree frogs are jumping out of the swamp and hopping all over everybody, squashing them flat or licking them up on their long sticky tongues and swallowing them. You have to zap them with a shrink ray to turn them back into frogspawn. You scoop them up in jam jars and put them back into the swamp. Only they don't want to go. They prefer being grown-up frogs and squashing people. And the swamp is full of alligators that try to eat you."

"Do you think you could all finish Zap Trap together?"

"I don't know. We never have before."

"Well, try," I said. "I'll help. If you can do it you might just save Earth."

"We'll try," Zik said.

My next job was to warn the world of what was going to happen when **ICARUS** succeeded – *if* they succeeded. I wasn't absolutely sure what that would be myself, though I could make a guess. Some kind of massive suck-down – like being on the end of a cosmic vacuum cleaner. But how to tell the world? I hadn't got a clue and neither had Tipperary. We went indoors to ask Aunt Doris for advice. That was a mistake.

"My advice to you, young man," Aunt Doris said, "is to go to bed and sleep on it."

"You don't understand, Aunt Doris. I haven't got *time* to sleep."

"You're a baby, Moses," Aunt Doris said. "Babies need their sleep. That's it and all about it."

And it was. I must have been very tired, because I slept deeply and dreamt of home. I woke suddenly with Tipperary sitting up beside me and Hector making a noise like ten dogs down in the kitchen.

"Getoutgetoutgetoutgetout!"

"Stay there, Moses," Tipperary said. As if I had any choice. She jumped out of bed and ran downstairs. I heard the back door open and Hector hurtled out into the dark yard, snarling. I heard someone running and then some very rude words. I'm learning quite a few of them. These ones sounded as though whoever said them was in pain. Next came a growl from Hector.

"StinkyStoatwarden!Hectorbiteharder nexttime!"

After that Tipperary locked all the doors and shut all the windows. When she came back up to bed she brought Hector with her. She climbed into bed and settled down beside me. Hector jumped on to her feet and made himself comfortable. Neither of them spoke.

"He was after me, wasn't he?" I said. "He knows."

12 Miracles

Aunt Doris made porridge for everyone next morning. We didn't talk about Silas Stoatwarden's nocturnal visit. Tipperary sat me in a high chair and fed me spoonfuls. Porridge is one thing I'm not going to miss when I've left this planet. If I ever do.

"One for Hector and one for me and one for the bus and one for Auntie Doris," she kept saying, but I had to eat all of them each time. In the end I grabbed the spoon and splatted Hector who was underneath the table. Hector likes porridge. He didn't mind being splatted. He just licked it off and tried to get hold of the spoon to splat me back.

"Stop it, you two," Aunt Doris said. "I'm pondering on how young Moses is going to warn the world."

We all waited in silence while Aunt Doris pondered.

Presently she spoke. "I always knew that you were something special, Moses," she said slowly. "But I doubt if anybody else is going to believe in you. They didn't listen to the other Moses at first and he wasn't saying anything half as daft as what you are. D'you know what he did to make them listen in the end?"

"What?"

"Miracles. That's what."

"What sort of miracles, Aunt Doris?"

Aunt Doris shook her head. "Don't they teach you anything at school?" she asked.

"They teach us physics. It's similar to miracles."

"Blow physics – miracles are what you want," Aunt Doris said. "Listen. Moses told Pharaoh to let his people go but Pharaoh wouldn't. Right? So Moses said, 'If you refuse to let them go, Pharaoh, behold, I will smite all thy borders with frogs.' And he did. There was frogs everywhere.

Frogs in the houses, frogs in the beds, frogs in the ovens, frogs in the kneading troughs."

"Sounds like *Zucchini*," I said. "What's a kneading trough?"

"Never you mind. Don't interrupt."

"What came after the frogs, Aunt Doris?" Tipperary asked.

"The plague of lice. After the plague of lice it was the swarms of flies. Then it was the murrain of beasts. All the Egyptians' animals took sick and died."

I told that bit to Hector. He was furious. **"Notfair!"** he growled from under the table. **"Rottenstinkingmeanmurrain!"**

"After the murrain of beasts came the plague of boils. Very nasty, I should think, especially in that heat. Then there was hail, locusts, darkness for three days and after that things got really bad."

"But what's that got to do with *our* Moses?" Tipperary asked.

"It's obvious, girl. Moses should do miracles! On the telly! That'll make 'em sit up and listen!"

"If Moses does miracles on telly they'll take him away and do experiments on him to find out how he did them. They'll find out he's an alien. I don't know what they'll do then, but it's sure to be nasty."

I thought of Silas Stoatwarden, and shivered. Tipperary picked me up and held me tight.

"Perhaps you're right, dear," Aunt Doris nodded. "Well then, let's try the newspapers instead. We won't say where we're ringing from. They can't take Moses away if they can't find him, can they?"

I could hear what happened next because Tipperary was holding me about two inches from the phone.

"Amanda Cassandra here. Newsdesk. Whoops! Would you hold the line? My pen has just floated out of the window. Digby darling, pass me another pen. Right. I'm all yours. Fire away."

"Listen carefully, Amanda Cassandra," said Tipperary. "Because I have an urgent message for you. You know this trouble we're having with gravity?"

"Do I, *darling*? There goes my lap top! *Quick,* Quentin! Catch it. Thank you, sweetie."

"Well, right here with me is the only person on Earth who knows how to put it right."

"Darling! Really? Too wonderful! Do tell!"

"He'll tell you himself."

Tipperary held the phone up for me while I told Amanda that I'd come to Earth in a space ship in order to save the planet, and that I'd more or less worked out how to do it, and that now I needed to warn everybody about what might happen when I did it. If I did it.

"When I set off the power surge," I said, "if I do, there's going to be a sudden Whoosh! and everybody will be sucked back down to Earth. So they'd better be ready for it."

Amanda Cassandra started to sniffle and snort. Pretty soon she was laughing out loud.

"Darling!" she shrieked. "Too, *too* funny! But not our sort of story!"

There was a click, and Amanda Cassandra was gone.

"OK," sighed Tipperary. "Let's try another."

Next she got through to Maurice Murgatroyd of the *Daily Disaster*. Right from the start he was drooling down the phone.

"Spaceship? *Sexy!*" he burbled. "Alien arrives to save the planet? That's my kind of story!

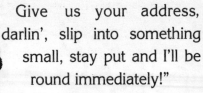

Give us your address, darlin', slip into something small, stay put and I'll be round immediately!"

"No address," Tipperary said. "Just print what I say."

"No address, no picture, baby doll. No picture, no story. No story, no dosh." He hung up.

"Never mind, pet," Aunt Doris said. "Who believes what they print in the *Daily Disaster* anyway?"

"It's got to be TV," I said, from under the table. "There's nothing else for it." I quite fancied going on TV.

13 Charley Cool

Just at first, the TV people were not too happy about coming out to the back of beyond to interview a talking baby. Nobody seemed to take us seriously. Not until Tipperary managed to get a word with Charley Cool.

You can tell by looking at him that Charley Cool is someone who has a good time whatever he's doing. Whoever's doing it with him has a good time too. He's mad about all kinds of exciting things and his favourite hobby is hang-gliding – he carries a fold-out wing and harness with him wherever he goes.

Charley Cool has dark skin and glossy brown

eyes and a lot of curly black hair, all springy and bouncy.

On Earth, hair seems to be very important. It can be straight or curly, thick or thin, spiky or floppy. Some people have lots and some have none. Most people spend a lot of time fluffing theirs up or slicking it down. Hector doesn't – he just licks his. At home everybody has short green hair and that's that, but we go to a lot of trouble to get our skin colour exactly right. Right now dark spinach is *the* thing. Last summer everybody had to be as pale as lettuce leaves.

"What a cool, cool day!" Charley said happily when Tipperary had introduced herself. "The whole world's gone crazy and it isn't even dinner time! Manchester United cancelled their home game last night because their ball went into orbit! This morning a racing pigeon from Doncaster broke the sound barrier, kilts have been banned in Glasgow and you've got a *talking baby*!! Brilliant! Totally fantastic! What can he say? Will he say something to me now?"

"He might," Tipperary said. "I'll ask him."

When she held the phone up for me I could hear Charley Cool talking to someone in the background.

"Put them away, Sylvester," he was saying. "The big one's hissing. I don't think she's too happy."

"Have you got snakes in your office, Charley Cool?" I asked.

"Five, little buddy. They were going to be on News Round but this gravity business is upsetting them. They keep walking round on their tails."

"What's he saying?" Aunt Doris whispered.

"He's got snakes in his office," I whispered back.

"*Snakes?*" whooped Aunt Doris. "*Snakes!!* Didn't the other Moses do something clever with a snake?"

"What sort of thing, Aunt Doris?"

"Turned it into a stick, I think," Aunt Doris said. "Or was it sticks into snakes? One or t'other."

"I could do better than that," I said.

"Whydon'tyouthenbig-head?" Hector asked.

"All right, dogslobber," I said. "I will."

I asked Charley Cool to come down and meet me and to bring the snakes with him.

"You want snakes? You got snakes," said Charley. "But why?"

"I've got to warn people," I explained. "About what's going to happen." I told him all about it and he didn't stop me or ask questions. When I said I wanted to talk to the snakes on TV so people would see I really could do weird things, he got seriously excited.

"Talk to one now," he begged. "Go on!"

"Put one on the phone, Charley," I said. I asked him to hold the phone close to the snake's ear – they do have ears, on the sides of their heads. Then I asked the snake to get the other four together and write **CRAZY** on the studio floor.

Charley came back on the phone gasping with amazement. "D'you think they could do my name?" he asked.

"Easy," I said. "Put the snake back on the phone."

"COOL!" Charley gasped. "Incredible!"

"Incredible's too long," I said. "How about BBC?"

The snakes wrote BBC. Charley went wild.

Tipperary told Charley where to meet us, and he said he'd be down right away with his team.

"Only bring people you trust," Tipperary warned him. "If word gets out where Moses is, his life will be in danger. As a matter of fact, it already is."

"I'll bring Kate on camera and Krishna on sound. And Sylvester, because the snakes won't come without him. They're safe. Trust me," said Charley.

Somehow, we did.

At midday we fetched the hens indoors to prevent them from floating away. Bess was very excited. She gave Hector a hard look, and he gave her one back. She flew up to the top of the dresser, knocked down two of Aunt Doris's favourite cups and laid an egg in the sugar bowl. Finally she perched on top of the grandfather clock and cleared her throat.

"Ladies," she began. "This is a grave and perilous hour. Only yesterday we experienced, for the first time, the joy and glory of true flight. Today we are in danger of soaring aloft into the stratosphere – which I believe to be a cold and draughty place and quite unsuitable for hens. Tomorrow – who knows? Outer space? Such may be our destiny. It may fall to hens to be the great explorers of the sky. But for now, Aunt Doris says we've got to stay indoors. So I suggest we settle down and have a quiet afternoon."

They had just settled down – perching on the backs of chairs, on the kitchen dresser, on windowsills and pelmets – when Charley Cool arrived with Sylvester and the snakes and unsettled them.

The team had had a difficult drive from London, owing to the peculiar gravitational conditions. People were loading their cars up with anything heavy they could find. Most of them were driving slowly but even so there were a lot of pile-ups on the motorway. Earth people are not good drivers. Perhaps it's because they don't do physics. Several cyclists who had not weighted themselves down properly were blown away and never found.

  Hector didn't look too happy when Sylvester and his snakes came through the door and one or two

hens panicked. "Help! Bess! Save us!" they squawked. "There's a giant chicken-eating worm and she's going to eat us up!"

Bess eyed the largest of the snakes with interest. "I doubt that," she said. "She doesn't look hungry to me. She looks upset."

"Ask her if she's hungry, Moses," Bess said, so I did.

The snake shook her head.

"Good," said Bess. "And when she *is* hungry, ask her what she likes to eat?"

"Weetabixsss," the snake hissed. *"With a little warm milk and sssugar pleasssse."*

I told the hens what she had said.

"It's all right, ladies," Bess called. "You can come down off the pelmets. She eats Weetabix, not hens."

In fact the snakes were all extremely shy. Only one of them – the largest one, who I'd already spoken to – was willing to talk to me. Her name was Sissy. Like most snakes, Sissy was a private, solitary creature who preferred to keep out of the limelight.

"There's so much gossip about us snakes," Sissy said. *"Serpents are sweet-natured and sincere citizens. Sadly, we seem to be seen instead as slimy, slithering sneaks. Us snakes are a sadly misunderstood species."*

I had to explain just how important it was for her to help me before Sissy could bring herself to agree to go on television. After that, it took her a good half an hour to coax Sukey, Suzette, Solomon and Sinclair to cooperate.

Charley Cool had brought all kinds of clobber with him – lights, cameras, recording equipment, even his hang-glider in its little backpack, because he never went anywhere without it. Also, Chinese take-aways and pots of baby-food, in case we had missed lunch. Bess and the hens ate up the prawn crackers and Hector had a whole spring roll, but all I got was babyfood. Babyfood tastes of absolutely nothing. If Earth babies could talk they would refuse to eat it.

After lunch, Krishna clipped a microphone to the front of my babygrow and asked me not to dribble. It's difficult, because I'm teething now and you just have to chew on something when you're teething. I couldn't help chewing on the microphone. Krishna mopped it and checked the sound again, while Kate put up her lights and did a few test shots. She explained that our faces would be made all fuzzy on the TV so viewers wouldn't recognise us.

When we were ready to roll, Charley stood up and patted his braids.

"Hi there," he said to camera. "This is Charley Cool bringing you a special interview from a *top secret* location. I'm here to meet an incredible talking baby. His name's Moses and he's got some unbelievable stuff to tell you, so listen up."

He winked at me and smiled at Tipperary. Tipperary blushed. Aunt Doris gulped. Bess hid behind the teapot and Hector shot under the sofa. Charley and I were the only ones who kept our cool.

"Tipperary," said Charley. "Will you tell me first how your dog Hector found Moses on top of a mountain?"

Tipperary told. Hector smirked.

"Incredible," murmured Charley, gazing into Tipperary's eyes. "Awesome. Fantastic. Unbelievable." But he wasn't talking about how Hector found me on the mountain.

Next, Aunt Doris told Charley how she'd

overheard me talking to Bess. Charley asked Bess to say a few words to me on camera, but she came over all panicky and hid under the tea cosy.

After that, I sat on Aunt Doris's lap and explained to the viewers that I had come from another planet to save the world and that I had until midnight to do it.

"Just one thing, Moses," Charley Cool asked when I'd finished. "How come there's a hole at the Pole? I mean, how did it *get* there, man?"

"It's a long story, Charley," I said. "And it isn't strictly relevant."

Hector made a rude noise from behind the sofa.

I sat on Tipperary's lap next, in case the viewers thought Aunt Doris was a ventriloquist, and explained about **ICARUS** and *Zucchini*.

"The Intercontinental **All Round Unbeatable Stars**, **ICARUS** for short," I began, "will be represented by the six world champion *Zucchini* players:

Irina from **Moscow**,
Mitch from **Chicago**,
Grace Miliswa from **Johannesburg**,

Ajaz from **London**,
Zik from **Lagos**,
and the champion of champions,
Sachiko from **Kyoto**."

"How exactly did you make contact with **ICARUS**?" Charley asked.

"On the net," I said. "Hector helped me."

"For those viewers who don't yet surf the net," Charley said, "I will just tell you that it's a world-wide computer club that anyone can join. Now – here's the important bit – **ICARUS** aim to finish playing *Zucchini* on the dot of midnight. Tell me, Moses – if everything works out, what's gonna happen then?"

"If my calculations are right, we'll generate a surge of electricity strong enough to reverse the polarity of the electrical charge in the molten magma at present escaping from the North Pole. This will cause it to be sucked back down into the centre of the Earth."

"**Wow**!" said Charley. "**Cosmic!**" But he wasn't listening to me. He was looking at Tipperary with a melting expression on his face and Tipperary was gazing back at him with the same dopey expression on hers.

Hector and I exchanged glances. Something was going on. I tapped the mike and Charley turned back to me.

"Sorry. You lost me there, Moses. You were getting technical," he said. "Can you make it simpler for me?"

"OK," I said. "There'll be a huge **thunk** at midnight."

"Could you define a **thunk**, Moses?"

"A **suck-down**."

"What exactly is a **suck-down**, Moses?"

"Everybody will feel very, very heavy. Everybody should lie down. Nobody should be up a ladder cleaning windows, or bungee-jumping, or rock-climbing, or hang-gliding, or driving a car or riding a bike, or deep-sea diving, or snow-boarding, or dancing. Even sitting on the loo could be a risky business."

Charley looked straight at camera. "It is *crucial* that you listen to this dude," he told the viewers. "And remember, **thunkdown** is midnight. One last thing, Moses. What happens if **ICARUS** *don't* finish play by midnight?"

"The Earth crumples up like a ball of paper and everyone falls off into outer space."

Charley cleared his throat. "I see," he said.

Finally I sat on Charley's lap and told everybody they should try to keep calm.

"It's not the end of the world," I said. "At least I hope it's not."

Charley turned back to the camera. "Detailed news flashes will keep you informed during the build-up to **thunkdown**," he said. "A final warning will be broadcast world-wide, at twenty

91

minutes to midnight Greenwich Mean Time. After that, we will broadcast a minute-by-minute countdown to gravitational normality. This is Charley Cool from News Round saying *good night* and *good luck.*"

And that was that. I couldn't help my nappy leaking.

When Charley had dried his jeans off, he went outside with Kate and Krishna to film Hector demonstrating the effect of the change in the gravitational constant in the back yard. Hector jumped as high as the chimneys. Behind his flying ears the sky was strangely misty. Far to the north a trace of silvery gas hovered on the horizon.

They say danger brings people closer together and something was certainly bringing Charley and Tipperary close. They just couldn't stop smiling at one another. Every now and then Charley would pat his braids and Tipperary would try to wipe the engine oil off her cheek with her sleeve.

Back indoors, I asked the snakes to write KATE and BBC and NEWS on the floor, while Kate filmed us and Krishna recorded me and Sissy hissing.

"Don't know what the fuss is all about," Bess muttered from underneath the tea cosy. "Bunch of overgrown earthworms showing off on the telly."

Hector seemed to agree.

Once the film was in the can, Charley, Kate and Krishna packed up.

"It's been a real pleasure meeting you, Moses," Charley said. "Even if you did wet my jeans." He pinched my cheek and shook hands with Aunt Doris.

Then he turned to Tipperary. "It's been fantastic meeting you," he beamed. "Can we meet again soon?"

"The sooner the better," Tipperary said. She leaned forward and kissed him on the lips! **Eugh! Yukkk**!!!

Hector shot out from under the table and bit Charley's leg. For once, I knew just how he felt.

15 strewth

Kate must have shot just a glimpse of the bus by accident while she was filming Hector jumping in the yard. I expect it was only on the screen for a second – but a second was obviously long enough for Silas Stoatwarden. He heard the interview, recognised the bus, phoned the press and swung into action. What happened next was scary.

It was evening and we were watching ourselves on the news. Everything was ready – we just had to wait till it was time for **ICARUS** to start playing *Zucchini*. We were all feeling quite excited.

"Isn't Charley gorgeous, Aunt Doris?" Tipperary said.

"You could do a lot worse than Charley Cool, my girl. He seems like a very nice lad," Aunt Doris agreed.

Suddenly we heard cars bumping up the lane. Doors slammed, shoes scrunched, Bess squawked, Hector barked and a pack of journalists banged on our door. They pushed and shoved and flashed their cameras and all yelled at once. They offered Aunt Doris any amount of money to let them take a picture of "the alien" and begged Tipperary to pose with me in her arms.

Maurice Murgatroyd was at the front of the scrum, waving his wallet.

"Come on, darlin'!" he yelped. "Show us the little green man! Give us a butchers and we'll make it worf yer while!"

"Push off!" Aunt Doris shouted through the letter box. "There's no alien here!"

"Oh yes there is!" shouted Murgatroyd. "We know there is! We've seen him on the telly!"

"Go away!" Aunt Doris shouted.

But they wouldn't go away. "We want the alien!" they yelled. "Give us the little green man!"

Suddenly Silas Stoatwarden strode up to the door. The journalists fell silent as he bent down and spoke quietly through the letterbox. "If you're in possession of an alien," he said, "you could all be in deadly danger. There's no knowing what he may do. My advice to you is to hand the creature over *immediately*. Medical science has a right to examine him. *I* have a right to examine him. ***I want the alien and I want him NOW!***"

Tipperary picked me up and held me tightly in her arms. "I won't let him take you, Moses," she promised. "I won't let anyone take you."

Hector put his nose to the crack under the door and gave his most blood-curdling growl.

"*Bigdogbigdogbigdogbigdog!*" Hector growled. Hector's OK when you're in a tight corner.

"**Strewth!**" we heard Maurice Murgatroyd gasp. "They've gotta Rottweiler in there!"

Aunt Doris peeped out through the letter box. "That creep Silas Stoatwarden's gone," she said. "But Murgatroyd has fetched a crate of whisky out of the boot of his car. Looks like him and his mates are settlin' in for the evening."

They were. Outside, the yard grew dark. Every now and then a camera flashed outside the window or somebody rattled the door, but we took no notice. We were busy making plans. When we were ready Aunt Doris opened the window a crack and passed out a basket containing one dozen bottles of elderflower wine. Elderflower wine was not the only thing the bottles contained because Aunt Doris had added a slug of her special sleeping potion to every bottle.

"Something to wet your whistles, boys, while we make up our minds," she called.

"Fank you, Ma'am," Murgatroyd answered. "Seen the light, eh? Why not pass the little blighter out right now?"

"All in good time," Aunt Doris said. "Hold

your horses."

We gave them about half-an-hour to finish up the elderflower wine. Then Hector crept out to reconnoitre. Hector can be pretty fearless when the chips are down.

He crept back in and told me that all the journalists were asleep in their cars, snoring like warthogs. I told Aunt Doris and Tipperary.

"Good drop of potion that," Aunt Doris mused.

I woke the hens and warned them that they must be absolutely silent during the next phase of our plan. We lined up by the back door. Tipperary was in front with the keys to **SOFTIE** in her hand. Hector was by her side, teeth bared and hackles bristling. Next came Aunt Doris with me clutched tightly in her arms. The hens came last, with Bess at the back to chase up stragglers.

We crossed the dark yard with utmost stealth. Once we were out in the field we pelted up to the spinney and piled on to **SOFTIE**. Bess counted the hens on board.

"I'm going to lay you down in Hector's basket, Moses dear," Aunt Doris told me. "You'll be safe in there and you can fiddle with your old computer whatnots to your heart's content."

I nodded. Hector licked my face. Dogslobber is something you get used to when you're a friend of his.

"Get in beside him, Hector," Aunt Doris said. "Stop him from getting jolted loose and flying about the bus. He's got to concentrate."

She laid me down gently in Hector's Comfy Dog-Eze basket, nudged a pillow in behind my back to prop me up, and put the remote in my hands. Her wrinkled old face looked worried but her eyes were steady. Hector climbed in and curled himself around me. Tipperary switched everything on. She set up the video conferencing facility.

All of us, even the hens, were absolutely silent, engrossed in the flickering screens where six world champions prepared to throw every last milligram of brain power into the game of Zucchini.

Suddenly we heard a shout. Down in the yard, Maurice Murgatroyd had woken up and seen the flicker of our screens.

Two dozen journalists tumbled out of their cars, empty bottles tinkling round their feet, and ran stumbling over the field.

16 Pok**aaarrrkkk!!!**

Tipperary did not waste a second. She started up the engine and **SOFTIE**'s doors swished shut.

At the very same moment a new pack of journalists surged into the yard. Off in the distance we heard the ominous rumbling of a large, tracked vehicle bumping down the lane.

"We want to see the spacebaby!" a dozen voices hollered. "Show us the sprog from outa space!"

I cuddled close to Hector and tried not to hear.

"Lemme**out!**" Hector barked furiously. "Lemmeoutlemmeoutlemmeout!Bitebite bite *bitebite!*"

Tipperary hurled **SOFTIE** across the field, through the yard and out into the lane, scattering journalists in all directions as she swung us round and down the hill. There were cars parked all down the lane. Tipperary pranged as many as she could, slicing off wing mirrors, bouncing off bumpers, doing as much damage as possible.

"They'll be after us any minute, Aunt Doris," she warned. "Better be ready for them."

"Hold tight, hens!" I called – it's more of a squawk than a call, in chicken. If you were to translate it, it would sound like:

"Pokaaarrr**kkk!!!**"

Tipperary put her foot down, and the powerful engine, built and maintained by her own skilful hands, swung us out on to the road. We were heading for a rendezvous with victory or defeat. I had to fix Earth's gravity and fix it fast – or this wonderful planet and everybody on it would be finished.

Looking up, I saw Tipperary's face lit by the lights from the dashboard as she stared ahead, frowning fiercely. She glanced at me for a second and winked.

"OK, egg-head?" she asked.

I nodded. I was glad of Hector's strong, sleek body curled around me, wedging me into the dog basket. It was eleven o'clock precisely. One hour till **thunkdown**... or one hour till doom.

I turned back to the video. "We're under attack," I told **ICARUS**. "Pay no attention to anything you see on your screens. I'm going to count you down now. **Thirty** seconds to go. **Twenty**... wait for it, Mitch... **Ten**... **Nine**... **Eight**... **Seven**... **Six**... steady, Grace Miliswa... **Five**... **Four**... **Three**... **Two**... **One**... ZERO!"

Six dozen giant hairy-legged spiders flashed on to the split screen of the video conferencing monitor. Terrified Zucchinoids fled in all directions and six super-players threw themselves into Spinner Dinner.

Meanwhile at the back of the bus, Aunt Doris had opened up the Emergency Exit. "This oughta get 'em," she grunted, hauling an economy size bottle of cooking oil off a shelf in the snack bar and slapping it down on the counter. She added a family size tin of golden syrup and twelve bumper boxes of rock hard mint-choc-chip from the freezer.

"All set, Tipperary!" she called.

"Hold fire, Aunt Doris!" Tipperary yelled, as she took us up on to the motorway.

"What's happening, Hector?" I asked. "Tell me what's happening!"

Hector craned his neck so he could see out of the window. He tugged with his strong white teeth at my babygrow and pulled me up higher so I could see too.

Racing up the hill behind us was a fleet of fast cars bristling with people, all brandishing telephoto lenses and yelling at the tops of their voices. Over the engines' roar I heard, "*Get the Alien!*"

Hector crouched back down beside me. "Hector get **them!**" he growled. "Hector get **Hectorbite!**"

"Hector," I said. "You're a brother."

Tipperary flicked on her tail lights and put her hand down on the horn. She swung us out into the fast lane and we shot down that motorway like a duck on ice.

Up on the video conferencing monitor, Zik gave us a wave. The last of his spiders gobbled up the last of his bluebottles. He adjusted his shades and dived into Shark Attack.

By now, there was a swarm of vehicles strung out behind us like angry wasps, their yellow headlights blazing. Tipperary kept her foot down on the accelerator until Exit Eleven flashed up on our left.

"Hang on, everybody!" she yelled. She slowed to seventy and took us bucketing down the slip road. We were heading for Mount Wrath.

Mitch fiddled with his lucky baseball glove and dodged a flying spiderweb. Irina polished her lucky rouble. Ajaz swung into Shark Attack, let two sharks slither out of his net and fell back down to Spinner Dinner.

Gears crunched and engines screamed behind

us as frantic drivers followed us off the motorway.

"Fire one, Aunt Doris!" Tipperary yelled.

Aunt Doris upended the bottle of cooking oil out of the Emergency Exit and poured a shining slick down on to the road. The first four vehicles glided over the glistening tarmac, skimmed the ditch, and nestled down into the hedge.

"Four down, plenty more to go!" she shouted happily.

Maurice Murgatroyd roared up behind us and she let fly at him with the tin of golden syrup. The tin shattered his windscreen, the lid flew off and a kilo of molten sugar coated his angry face, causing him to leave the road and sail over the hedge into a field of barley.

"Lick that!" Aunt Doris cried happily.

"Slow down, Sachiko," I scolded, as she shot through Shark Attack and into Zap Trap. "You're too far ahead of the others. Zik, fetch a new shark net. Drag it with the cursor. Good lad."

Nobody spoke for a while, apart from Irina who said "**чёрт**!"- which is a rude word in Russian.

"Don't worry," I told her. "You're doing fine. Relax." She made a face at me and I smiled back at her.

A squad of bikers came up close behind us, their faces hidden behind helmets and goggles. "Give us the alien!" they yelled. "We want a scoop!"

"Try a scoop of this,boyos!" Aunt Doris yelled back. One dozen boxes of rock-hard mint-choc-chip bounced off one dozen helmets. One dozen rock-hard bikers sailed gracefully from their bikes and floated gently down into the soft grass by the roadside, groaning.

17 Ambush

I won't deny that it was fun, the bus chase. That
is, until they caught us.

Some of them must have nipped round
ahead somehow and ended up in front of us.
They'd felled a tree across the road and they
were waiting for us with their lights turned off as
we swung round the corner.

They'd chosen their spot well. With a cliff on
one side and a precipice on the other Tipperary
had no choice. She jammed on her airbrakes
and **SOFTIE** ploughed majestically into the tree
trunk with a sound of splintering wood.

"Holy Moley!" Tipperary gasped. "What have

107

I done to my paintwork?"

Headlamps pierced the darkness as several people jumped forward and began banging on the windows. Every time they jumped they rose into the air and bobbed angrily before drifting back down to the ground. One of them spotted Hector in front of the video monitor and shouted. Faces pressed against the window.

Grace Miliswa, glancing at the video conferencing screen, caught sight of them for a second and lost concentration, but only for a moment. Mitch stuck his tongue out. Irina frowned. Zik didn't spare them a glance. Zik just played.

Hector bared his teeth and snarled. The faces drew back, but only for a second.

"He's turned into a dog!" somebody shouted. **"The alien's turned into a dog!"**

"Grace Miliswa," I said quietly, "that was a lovely move. Well done. Slow down a little, Mitch. Stay cool. Don't rush yourself. Zik – keep doing what you're doing."

Aunt Doris locked the Emergency Exit and ran up the aisle. She crouched down beside Hector's basket, with an arm round each of us and glared at the faces outside.

"They won't get their hands on you, Moses," she promised. "Nor you neither, Hector."

Hector drew his lips back from his teeth and growled dog insults at the window.

Tipperary stayed at the wheel and kept the engine running. She looked out over the bobbing heads of the journalists as though none of them were there.

I turned back to the split screen. There were tree frogs everywhere. Zik had already frogspawned most of his, but Grace Miliswa was having trouble with her shrink ray. She kept shrinking people instead of frogs.

Four young men with crowbars were trying to smash their way through the toughened glass right beside Tipperary. She sat still with one eye on the wing mirror and the other on the rev counter, trying to find a gap in the crowd so we could make a getaway. There was no gap. They had already rolled a big log up behind us. We were stuck.

I don't know how things would have turned out if Charley Cool had not turned up in the nick of time in the BBC Outside Broadcasts van and skidded to a halt. He jumped out with Sylvester by his side.

Coiled around Sylvester's neck was Sissy, the largest of the snakes. Sylvester knew, and I knew, that the only thing Sissy would attack was a bowl of Weetabix. The people with the crowbar did *not* know that.

"Stand back!" Sylvester said. "Sissy is an Amazonian Liana Viper. She can spit venom right across a forest glade. She can spit round corners and up trees. One spot of her spit will stun a charging jaguar. Any sudden noise will make her spit. Or any sudden movement!"

The young men put down their crowbars and moved carefully back from the bus.

"Now, shift that log," Charley ordered.

"But they've got the alien in the bus!" somebody whispered.

"Rubbish!" Charley replied.

"How the bloomin' heck do *you* know?" somebody muttered.

"Because I've just come from filming an interview with him. You've missed your scoop. Go home."

"Not without the little green fella."

Sylvester took a few steps towards the nearest group of journalists and Sissy hissed her most nervous *hissssssss*. The young men bent down, and with some quiet grunts and groans, heaved the log out of the road.

"Good lass," said Sylvester, tickling Sissy under her chin, when he and Charley were safely aboard **SOFTIE**. Sissy said nothing. For a shy and retiring Liana Viper to be faced with a pack of rampaging journalists is not a pleasant experience. Sissy had gone into shock.

"Hello again, dear," Bess said. "Nice to see you." Sissy smiled, but did not speak.

Charley was giving Tipperary a kiss. I was just getting back to **ICARUS** and Aunt Doris was telling Charley to stop kissing Tipperary and let her drive the bus when a *horrible* thing happened.

A large tank lumbered round a bend in the road. It drove right up behind us and nudged **SOFTIE**'s back bumper with the barrel of its gun. A little round hole in the top opened up and Silas Stoatwarden stuck his head out.

"Holy Moley!" Tipperary gasped. "The crazy man's back!"

"Good evening," said Silas Stoatwarden, adding his horrible smile. "I suppose you realise that you are obstructing the public highway? What is more, you appear to be refusing to hand over a prisoner who belongs, not to you, but to science. *To science and to ME! I want him! Give him to me! Hand him over now or I'll push you off the cliff!"*

"You wouldn't..." faltered Aunt Doris.

"Man, you *couldn't*..." gasped Charley Cool.

"Oh yes I *could!*" smiled Silas Stoatwarden.

He inched his tank forward and we felt ourselves judder towards the very brink of the precipice. In a matter of seconds we would be over the edge.

"Open the door, Tipperary!" shrieked Aunt Doris. "Grab Moses and run for it!"

"Open the window!" I shouted. "Pass me out! Hand me over! He's going to push us all off the cliff!"

"Hang in there! shouted Charley. "I've gotta plan! Throw the ballast overboard!"

Aunt Doris, helped by Hector, heaved sacks of sand and cement out of the back window. Some of them landed on Silas Stoatwarden's tank, but not enough to stop him. Gradually, with a noise like boiling ballbearings, the tank inched forward.

Charley meanwhile, was easing himself out through one of **SOFTIE**'s little roof windows. It was a good thing he was skinny. Even so he only just made it because of his backpack. He climbed up and stood on the roof of the bus, wedging his large expensive trainers firmly into the opening he had just squeezed through. He whipped something out of the small backpack and shrugged it on. He pressed a little button, and a bright orange bat wing opened with a snap above his head. It furled and fluttered in the updraught like a giant jellyfish. The champion hang-glider was about to make the most dangerous flight of his life.

So were we.

The front half of the bus hung out over a sheer drop that ended in a swirl of mist deep in the valley below. Air travel is all very well in a plane but it's another matter in a bus, even without the force of gravity pulling you down to Earth. Whatever was going to happen next, I didn't want to see it. I shut my eyes and hid my face in Hector's neck.

There was a sudden, heart-stopping lurch. Then we all felt that magical moment that occurs when something large and heavy leaves the ground. "Is this really happening? Can this be true?" you ask yourself, as you are lifted up into the sky.

It was. **SOFTIE** soared free into the empty air, supported by Charley Cool's mighty orange bat wing.

"Hoooowheeeeeeeeeeey!" cried Charley joyfully. "YaaahooooooOOO!! Whayhaaaaay!!! This is *really* flying, man!!!"

There was a grinding sound behind and below us, as Silas Stoatwarden tried desperately to put his tank into reverse. Too late. I opened my eyes in time to see him plummeting to his doom.

SOFTIE soared on.

The flight lasted only minutes but it was strangely timeless. Charley, steering by a system of wires and pulleys that operated little ailerons, brought us skilfully round on to a current of warm air that was rising from the valley below. Up we soared, the thermal carrying us ever higher.

Far, far below a little puff of smoke showed where Silas Stoatwarden had gone to meet his maker. Or possibly the other fellow.

On our left, the mountain pearled and shimmered in the moonlight. On our right the night sky stretched away for ever, sifted with twinkling stars. I glanced at the clock on the dashboard. It was nearly midnight.

If **thunkdown** didn't happen dead on midnight, this lovely planet would be gone. And if **SOFTIE** was still aloft by thunkdown we were doomed.

18 Thunkdown

I fixed my eyes on the split screen of the big computer on which six games of *Zucchini* were drawing to a close. The time was five minutes to midnight.

Sachiko had got her shrink ray sorted and all her frogs were wriggling dots in jelly. Grace Miliswa looked calm and confident. Mitch was hovering just outside the tree frog jungle. He and Ajaz pushed the hair out of their eyes at precisely the same moment and leaned closer to their screens. Irina hummed and wriggled her eyebrows. Only Zik looked totally in control. He was swatting frogs around his screen and scooping frogspawn into jam jars and eating a mango, all at the same time.

I glanced at the clock on **SOFTIE**'s dashboard. "Sixty seconds to go," I said in a calm voice.

"That's cool," said Mitch.

"Fifty."

"I'm ready," Sachiko murmured modestly.

"Forty. Everyone sit down."

"What's happening to you, Moses?" Grace Miliswa asked. "It looks as though you're flying."

"Thirty. We are. Relax, everyone."

Irina gave a final wiggle to her eyebrows, clicked her mouse, and sat back to wait for midnight.

"Twenty."

Ajaz struggled with a last blob of frogspawn, dropped it, caught it again, and lobbed it home with a splash into a jungle pool.

Charley swung **SOFTIE** round and headed us straight into the mountain. He slid us in between two openings in an overhanging cliff and set us down on smooth, short grass. A perfect landing. The bus rolled to a halt like a giant roller skate and Charley dived off the roof.

"Ten seconds," I said. "Zik?"

Zik was on to his third mango.

"Nine. What's up, Zik?"

"My mouse got sticky. Must be the mangoes."

Zik finished his mango and played the last move of the game.

"**Zero!!!**" I shouted. "**Thunkdown!!!!**"

Everybody, all over the world, felt the most extraordinary sensation. Have you ever been the last person on the chain in a game of Snap the Whip? When everybody holds hands, and makes a long long line all round the playground, and they start turning round, and turning round, and the person at the front of the chain is just revolving on the spot, while the person on the end is whizzing round with their feet off the ground and their insides out?

That's what it felt like.

A surge of power shot out of the internet. There was a flash of lightning like no storm you've ever seen and a noise like two marbles the size of planets clicking together. The power whizzed once round the circumference of the Earth, shot up to the North Pole and hovered, fizzing for a moment high above the frozen sea, then locked on to the fountain of vaporised magma.

I managed to click on to the news channel just before I dropped the remote, and there on the

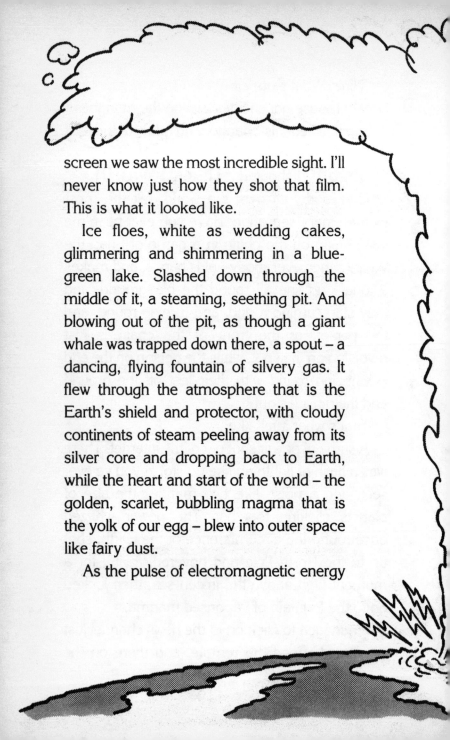

screen we saw the most incredible sight. I'll never know just how they shot that film. This is what it looked like.

Ice floes, white as wedding cakes, glimmering and shimmering in a blue-green lake. Slashed down through the middle of it, a steaming, seething pit. And blowing out of the pit, as though a giant whale was trapped down there, a spout – a dancing, flying fountain of silvery gas. It flew through the atmosphere that is the Earth's shield and protector, with cloudy continents of steam peeling away from its silver core and dropping back to Earth, while the heart and start of the world – the golden, scarlet, bubbling magma that is the yolk of our egg – blew into outer space like fairy dust.

As the pulse of electromagnetic energy

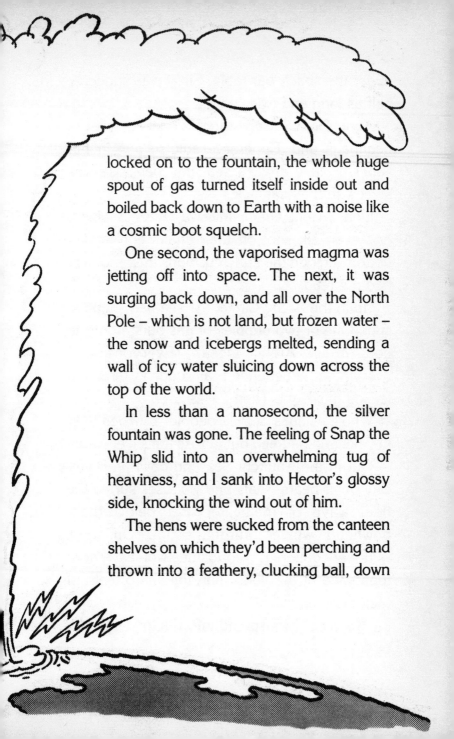

locked on to the fountain, the whole huge spout of gas turned itself inside out and boiled back down to Earth with a noise like a cosmic boot squelch.

One second, the vaporised magma was jetting off into space. The next, it was surging back down, and all over the North Pole – which is not land, but frozen water – the snow and icebergs melted, sending a wall of icy water sluicing down across the top of the world.

In less than a nanosecond, the silver fountain was gone. The feeling of Snap the Whip slid into an overwhelming tug of heaviness, and I sank into Hector's glossy side, knocking the wind out of him.

The hens were sucked from the canteen shelves on which they'd been perching and thrown into a feathery, clucking ball, down under the snack bar table. Sissy was suddenly half as long and twice as fat.

Aunt Doris disappeared under a pile of beanbags and Tipperary sank so low in her super de luxe driver's seat that her nose was level with the gearstick.

Irina, Mitch, Grace Miliswa, Ajaz, Sachiko, and even Zik shot off their chairs and landed bottom-first on the fluffy cushions their mothers had put ready.

Up in the Arctic Circle, the sea bed snapped shut. One or two bubbles of gas burst from the cold green Arctic Ocean. Everyone and everything experienced a sudden, terrifying feeling of weight. Then it was over.

Whole villages of Inuit people launched their kayaks and paddled out across the silver water.

Out in the Chukchi Sea and down in Baffin Bay polar bears, seals and walruses surfed the tidal wave of meltwater. Far below them bowhead whales surged south. On land, reindeer galloped alongside wolves, more frightened of the flood than the sharp teeth of their hunters.

"*It's over,*" I whispered into Hector's ear. "*It's over.*"

19 Goodbye, Earth

"Well," said Aunt Doris, struggling out from underneath the beanbags and helping Bess up on to the table top.

"Well." She patted Hector, and lifted me out of the dog basket. She felt me all over, carefully.

"Well," she said again, and peeped at the monitor.

In Kyoto, Sachiko was smoothing down her jeans and patting her glossy black hair.

All we could see of Irina in Moscow was her bottom, as she searched under her desk for her lucky rouble.

Mitch was doing a victory dance round his

lucky baseball glove.

Ajaz was kissing his mother, but stopped when he saw us looking.

Grace Miliswa was standing very straight, blushing like mad. She was listening to someone on the telephone. "Thank *you*, Mr President," she said. "It was nothing really."

Over in Lagos, Zik was polishing his shades.

"Well," said Aunt Doris for the fourth time, and I realised she didn't know what else to say – which doesn't often happen to Aunt Doris.

Out on the grass, Tipperary untangled herself for a moment from Charley Cool's embrace. "I think it's time we got Moses back to his dad," she said.

"D'you know the way?" Charley asked. "Can you drive?"

"Charley Cool, if you can fly this bus, I can certainly drive her," Tipperary told him.

She took us as high up the mountain as we could go. Then we got out and walked until we reached the place where two jagged points of rock stand under a tall pine tree.

The air was clear. The moon was round and fat and amber, like a traffic light. The far off stars trembled against the deep blue sky. When

Tipperary held me up to look at them, I felt kind of homesick.

She put me on the ground, holding my two hands so I wouldn't fall. I stood up, taking all my weight on my legs and she let go, keeping her hands close to mine so I could grab them if I wanted to. That's when I took my first four steps on Earth. It felt wonderful.

"Notbad," Hector said. "Especiallywithonly twolegs.Nowtrytotakealeakwithoutfallingover."

Charley opened a bottle of champagne he happened to have with him in his wonderful backpack, and we drank a toast to gravity, love and friendship.

I sat on Tipperary's lap, leaning back against her and looking at the sky. One of her strong hands was curled round my shoulder so I wouldn't slip if I began to nod off. The other held my feet and gently stroked my ten toes. Charley sat beside us, sipping champagne and humming quietly.

The circle of bright light came in over the mountain and turned the tree tops violet, indigo, azure, emerald, golden, orange and ruby red. The noise dropped and the colours faded.

Charley and Sylvester thought the spaceship was a meteor at first. They thought it was going to crash into the side of the mountain and blow us all to bits. I couldn't think of anything except how beautiful it was. Smooth and shimmering, silver and shining, with a vibration you could hear and feel and see and smell.

I stood up, wobbling between Tipperary and Aunt Doris while the mountain shook and Hector howled, Bess did her best to keep the hens calm and Sissy clung to Charley.

The ship floated down and settled right beside us, a smooth, fat pod, rocking slightly on its belly in the grass. The top opened and Dad came fizzing out. He rearranged his body to make it look like ours, so as not to frighten anybody. He took me gently out of Tipperary's arms.

At first I thought he'd speak to me, but then I

remembered. We don't talk. We just think. So I thought.

"I did it, Dad."

"Good lad," my dad thought back. I smiled, and he smiled and I knew that he understood about everything that had happened down on Earth.

"Dad," I thought, "can Hector and Tipperary and Aunt Doris come back with us? Just for a little while? Please, Dad?"

"Would you like to visit with us?" Dad asked them. He asked out loud because they couldn't hear him thinking.

"Space travel? Why not?" said Tipperary.

"What about you, Aunt Doris?"

"I'll come," Aunt Doris decided. "Provided the hens can come as well."

"Hector?" Dad asked. "You too?"

"Yes!Yess!! **Yesss!!!**" Hector barked, bouncing up and down on the spot.

So that's how it was.

The hens were very little trouble. Coming from eggs, they understood metamorphosis. Hector was more of a problem. He said he didn't want to dematerialise and how did he know we'd put him back together the right way round, and were there bones in outer space, and could he bring his basket and other daft things. But in the end he shut his eyes and came.

Tipperary and Charley said goodbye, though only for a little while. I could see that Charley wanted to come with us, but Tipperary told him that although she liked him a lot, she felt they hadn't known each other long enough to go off into space together.

She gave him **SOFTIE**'s keys and told him to keep the engine running smoothly. She kissed him. Then she took Aunt Doris's hand and they went up together.

Charley climbed into the bus with Sylvester. He blew his nose and wiped his eyes and hummed a little tune. I don't know if he knew what he was humming. It was an old tune, one I'd heard Aunt Doris sing. He began to sing the words, quietly. "*It's a long way to Tipperary...*"

He looked at me, and winked, and waved goodbye.

I stood alone for a few minutes, looking down at the grass and up at the sky, waiting for the silver pod to open for me.

Then I felt myself go bubbly, and the grass under my toes became a thousand points of light, and I was gone.